D0618962

THIS WALKER BOOK BELONGS TO:

For
Catherine and Sarah

First published 1990 by Walker Books Ltd
87 Vauxhall Walk, London SE11 5HJ

This edition published 1991
Reprinted 1992

Printed and bound in Hong Kong by
South China Printing Co. (1988) Ltd

British Library Cataloguing in Publication Data
West, Colin
Go tell it to the toucan.
I. Title
823'.914 [J]
ISBN 0-7445-1785-0

Go tell it to the toucan

Written and illustrated by

Colin West

WALKER BOOKS
LONDON

Hey, today it is my birthday!
thought the elephant one morning.
I'll go tell it to the toucan,
so then he'll tell everybody
all about my birthday party,
and we'll have a jamboree!

So Old Jumbo looked around him
but he couldn't find the toucan,
so instead he told the tiger:
"Hey, today it is my birthday!
Please go tell it to the toucan,
so then he'll tell everybody
all about my birthday party,
and we'll have a jamboree!"

So the tiger looked around him
but he couldn't find the toucan,
so instead he told the warthog,
and the warthog told the hippo:

"Hey, today is Jumbo's birthday!
Please go tell it to the toucan,
so then he'll tell everybody
all about the birthday party,
and we'll have a jamboree!"

So the hippo looked around him
but he couldn't find the toucan,
so instead he told the lion,
and the lion told the bullfrog,
and the bullfrog told the zebra:

"Hey, today is Jumbo's birthday!
Please go tell it to the toucan,
so then he'll tell everybody
all about the birthday party,
and we'll have a jamboree!"

So the zebra looked around him
but he couldn't find the toucan,
so instead he told the rabbit,
and the rabbit told the rhino,
and the rhino told the lizard,
and the lizard told the panda:

"Hey, today is Jumbo's birthday!
Please go tell it to the toucan,
so then he'll tell everybody
all about the birthday party,
and we'll have a jamboree!"

So the panda looked around him
but he couldn't find the toucan,
so instead he told the ostrich,
and the ostrich told the tortoise,
and the tortoise told the cricket,
and the cricket told the leopard,
and the leopard told the monkey:

"Hey, today is Jumbo's birthday!
Please go tell it to the toucan,
so then he'll tell everybody
all about the birthday party,
and we'll have a jamboree!"

So the monkey looked around him
and upon the highest treetop
at long last he found the toucan!
So the monkey told the toucan
what Old Jumbo told the tiger
what the tiger told the warthog
what the warthog told the hippo
what the hippo told the lion
what the lion told the bullfrog
what the bullfrog told the zebra
what the zebra told the rabbit
what the rabbit told the rhino
what the rhino told the lizard
what the lizard told the panda
what the panda told the ostrich
what the ostrich told the tortoise
what the tortoise told the cricket
what the cricket told the leopard
what the leopard had just told him:

"Hey, today is Jumbo's birthday!
So please go tell everybody
all about the birthday party,
and we'll have a jamboree!"

So the toucan looked around him...

and he looked behind the bushes...

and he looked among the flowers...

and he looked down by the river...

And the toucan looked all over,
but he still could find nobody,
so he went to tell Old Jumbo
there could be no jamboree...

But when the toucan found him,
"Hey, hello there!" cried Old Jumbo.
"Thanks for telling everybody
all about my birthday party...

"You're a really clever toucan.
Come and join the...

JAMBOREE!"

MORE WALKER PAPERBACKS
For You to Enjoy

Also by Colin West

THE KING OF KENNELWICK CASTLE
illustrated by Anne Dalton

It's raining, and the King of Kennelwick Castle is feeling glum.
But here comes a page to cheer him up with a parcel
from the Queen of Spain herself.

"Splendid cumulative story… Novice readers will enjoy this one."
British Book News
ISBN 0-7445-1414-2 £2.99

JUNGLE TALES

Simple, but colourful cumulative stories, each with a twist in the tail.
Ideal for early readers

"Have you seen the crocodile?"	ISBN 0-7445-1065-1	£3.99
"Hello, great big bullfrog!"	ISBN 0-7445-1227-1	£2.99
"Not me," said the monkey	ISBN 0-7445-1228-X	£3.99
"Pardon?" said the giraffe	ISBN 0-7445-1229-8	£2.99